For Amelia Swan—the girl
who loves to dance!
Eccl 3:4
—J.D. & K.D.

Pete the Cat and the Cool Cat Boogie
Text copyright © 2017 by Kimberly and James Dean
Illustrations copyright © 2017 by James Dean
All rights reserved. Printed in the United States of America.
No part of this book may be used or reproduced in any manner whatsoever without written
permission except in the case of brief quotations embodied in critical articles and reviews.
For information address HarperCollins Children's Books, a division of HarperCollins Publishers,
195 Broadway, New York, NY 10007.
www.harpercollinschildrens.com
ISBN 978-0-06-240434-3 [trade bdg.]
ISBN 978-0-06-240909-6 [lib. bdg.]
The artist used pen and ink with watercolor and acrylic paint on 300lb press paper to create the
illustrations for this book.
Typography by Jeanne L. Hogle
17 18 19 20 21 PC 10 9 8 7 6 5 4 3 2 1
❖
First Edition

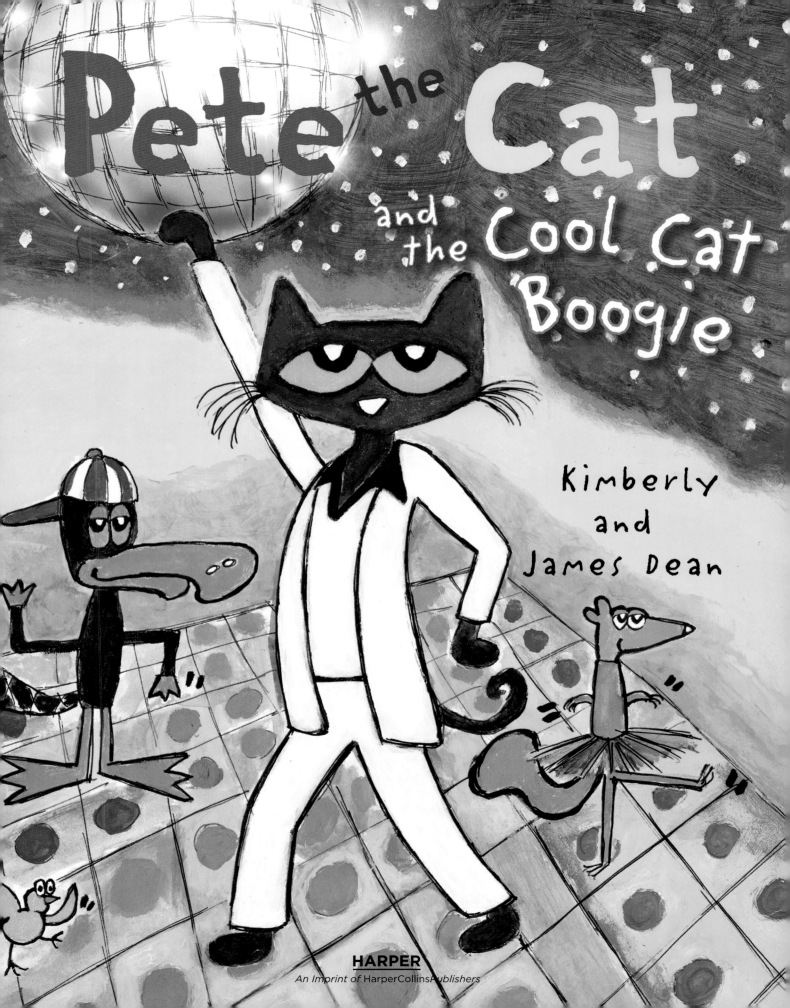

Pete the Cat

and the Cool Cat Boogie

Kimberly and James Dean

HARPER

An Imprint of HarperCollins Publishers

Pete the Cat was learning a new dance—the COOL Cat Boogie!

Then Grumpy Toad came along.

"I really dig that song but Pete, you dance all wrong!"

Pete did not know what to say. He just turned and walked away.

Pete couldn't sleep at all that night!
"What if Grumpy Toad was right?
What if my moves are bad?"
The thought of NOT dancing made
Pete feel sad.

"Dancing is like magic!
When I hear a groovy beat
I'm full of happy in my feet!

Pete was practicing the Cool Cat Boogie
when he saw Squirrel.
  "Hey, Squirrel,

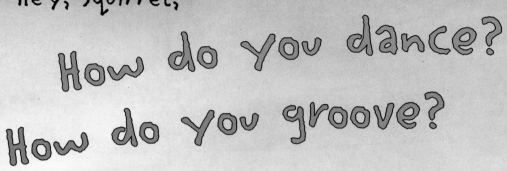

How do you dance?
How do you groove?

Can you teach me how to move?"

"Ahhhh!

Ouch! Pete, you stepped on my toes!

That's not how this dance goes!"

Pete did not know
what to say.
He just turned
and walked away.

"But dancing is like magic! When I hear
a groovy beat I'm full of HAPPY in my feet!

I won't give up!
I love to dance.

Let me give it one more chance."

Pete was still practicing the Cool
Cat Boogie when Gus came along.

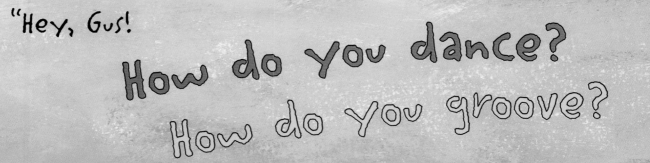

"Sure, Pete!
It's a simple song.

Just do the robot and
dance along!"

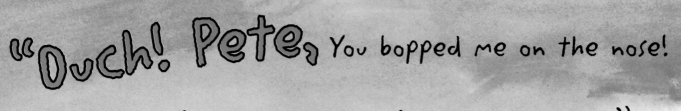

Pete did not know
what to say. He just
turned and walked away.

"But dancing is like magic!

When I hear a groovy beat I'm full of HAPPY in my feet!

I won't give up!

I love to dance.

Let me give it one more chance."

Pete was still trying to do the Cool Cat Boogie when Turtle came along.

Pete felt like giving up.

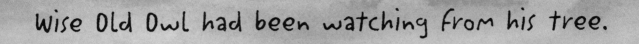

Wise Old Owl had been watching from his tree.

"Pete, it doesn't matter how you move
as long as you are being you!"

"You are right!!! I never want to miss a chance to dance!"

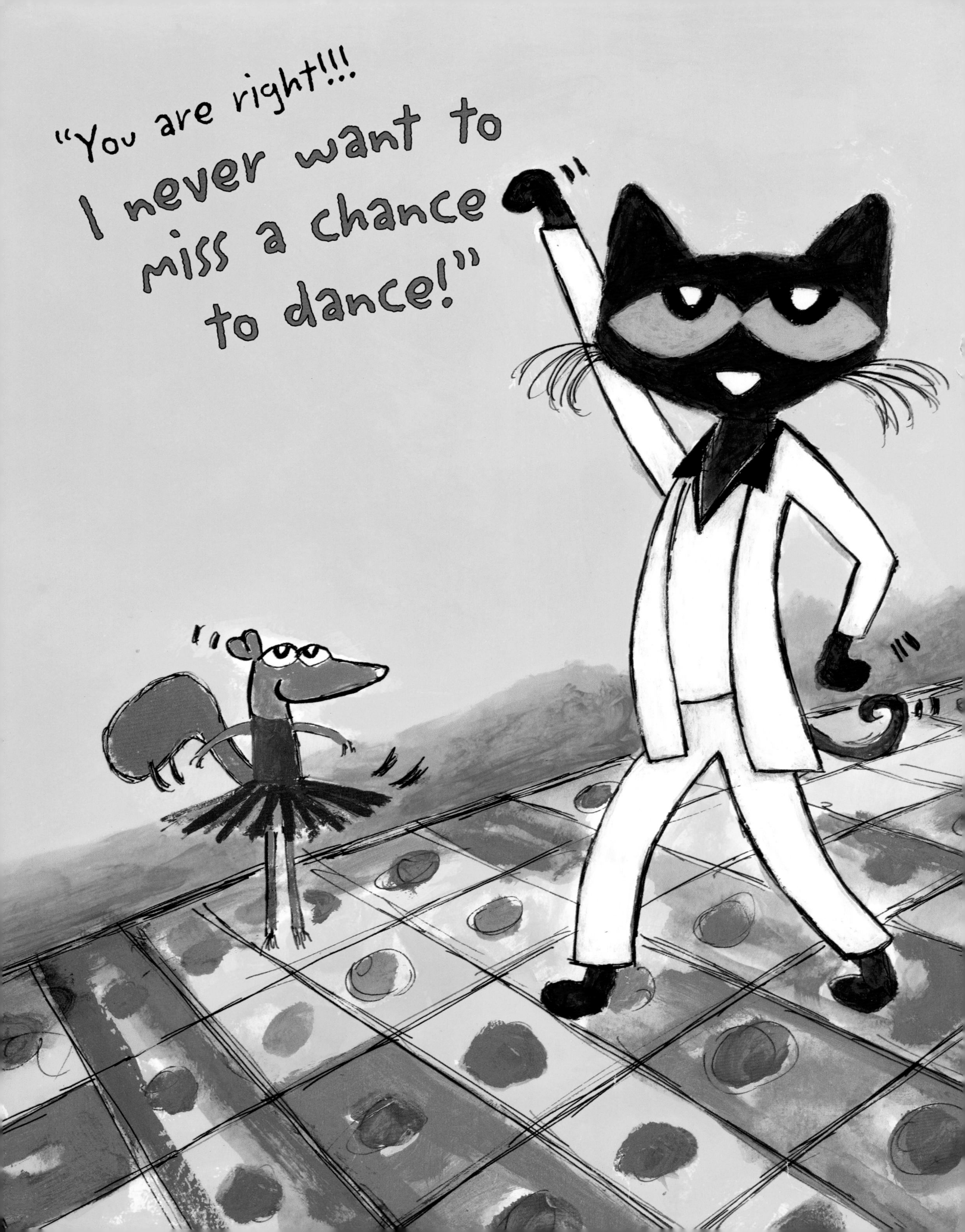

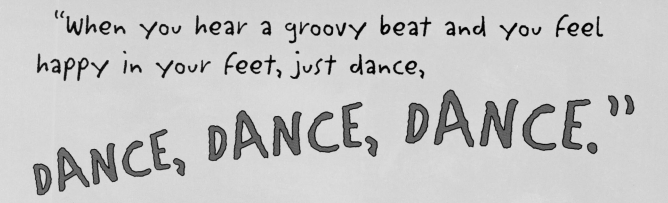

"When you hear a groovy beat and you feel happy in your feet, just dance,

DANCE, DANCE, DANCE."

Cool Cat Boogie

I want to boogie with you.
Grab your boogie shoes!

1.

2.

slide right...shake your tail

slide left...shake your tail

5.

6.

7.

rock and roll

jump back

rock and roll